The Winter Cave

First published in 2009
by Wayland

This paperback edition published in 2010 by Wayland

Text copyright © Penny Dolan 2009
Illustration copyright © Kirsten Richards 2009

Wayland
338 Euston Road
London NW1 3BH

Wayland Australia
Level 17/207 Kent Street
Sydney, NSW 2000

Series Editor: Louise John
Editor: Katie Powell
Cover design: Paul Cherrill
Design: D.R.ink
Consultant: Shirley Bickler

A CIP catalogue record for this book is available from the British Library.

ISBN 9780750257411 (hbk)
ISBN 9780750260374 (pbk)

Printed in China

Wayland is a division of Hachette Children's Books,
an Hachette UK Company

www.hachette.co.uk

The Winter Cave

Written by Penny Dolan
Illustrated by Kirsten Richards

WAYLAND

It was early evening, and the sun was setting over the camp. While Ma prepared dinner, Erg and his sister, Luli, played by the fire.

A fierce wind whistled through the forest. As the autumn trees shivered and shook, Grandpa listened.

"There's a storm headed this way," he said. "We must take shelter!"

Before long, big clouds came rolling across the sky. The forest grew darker than night itself.

Erg, Luli and all the tribe huddled inside their animal skin shelters, waiting for the storm to pass.
The wind howled angrily, the cold rain fell, and the trees moaned.

The next morning, although the storm had passed, Grandpa looked worried.

"The weather is changing. Soon we'll have to move to the cave for the winter. We must start gathering all we need."

"Ma, shall we go and look for berries?"
asked Luli.

"That's a good idea, children. We'll need
all the food we can find," said Ma, "but
don't stray too far."

Erg and Luli ran into the forest.
Suddenly, they stopped in the middle of
a clearing. A giant tree had fallen, and
its branches stretched across their path.

"The storm must have blown it over!"
said Erg. "And look, there's an
enormous hole where the roots have
been ripped from the ground!"

"The hole is full of yellow mud!
Look how sticky it is!" said Erg,
and he smeared a stripe of mud
across Luli's face.

"Urgh!" Luli cried. "I'll get you now!"

Luli chased Erg through the trees. She
caught up with him and streaked the
mud across his face.

"Now you've got mud whiskers, too!"
she said.

"I know! Let's turn ourselves into wild
animals!" said Erg.

"That's a great idea!" Luli laughed.

They drew spots along their arms and
stripes around their legs.

As the children raced back into camp, Ma chuckled, "I always knew you two were wild animals!"

"Where did you find that yellow mud?" asked Grandpa, who had returned from the forest, with some small bundles tied round his waist.

Erg and Luli led Grandpa to the fallen tree, where he scooped some of the mud into a piece of hollow wood.

"Go straight back home, children. I have something important to do," he told them.

Grandpa walked through the forest until he arrived at the cave that his family would inhabit during the cold winter days. Striking a spark from his flint stone, he lit a wooden torch and went inside.

Grandpa untied the small bundles in which he'd wrapped berries, leaves, soil, wood ash and the bright yellow mud the children had discovered.

Grandpa took the different ingredients and, using grease from animal skins, mixed his chosen colour paints.

Grandpa felt the walls of the cave, carefully deciding which animal he would paint on the curves of the rock.

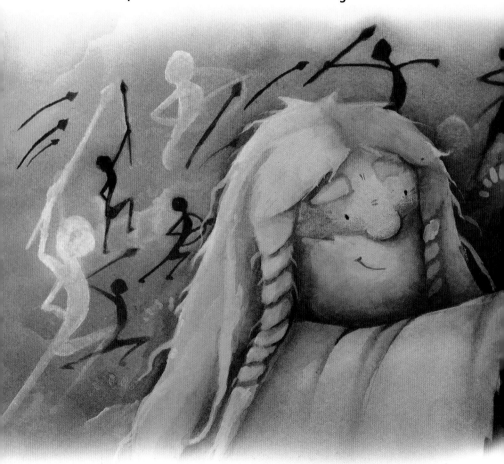

"A boar? No, some deer!" said Grandpa at last, and he set to work.

"If I paint well," Grandpa thought, "the gods will send deer to our hunting grounds next year." Grandpa began to draw a herd of deer leaping through the trees.

"We must remember how to hunt well, too," thought Grandpa. So he added people with spears, hunting the deer through the forest.

Grandpa worked through the night by the light of his burning torch. The flames lit up the cave walls, revealing creatures painted by Grandpa's own father, grandfather and other fathers long, long before.

Eventually he finished, tired, but proud of his work.

"Good!" he said. "I hope these paintings will please the gods."

When the first snowflakes began
to fall, the tribe knew winter
had finally arrived. They packed
up their belongings.

"Time to set off for the winter cave,"
Ma said.

"I can't wait to get there," cried Erg, who was dancing about with delight.

"Me, neither!" called Luli, jumping about, too.

Inside the cave, Ma and the aunts
spread out the bedding and food.
Pa and the uncles lit a fire just inside
the entrance to keep hungry wild
animals at bay.

The long dark days of winter had
come and there was no room to play
in the cave.

"I'm cold and hungry," grumbled Erg.
"I wish we could be camping outside
under the sky."

"What if the sun never comes back? Will
we have to live here forever?" worried Luli.

Grandpa heard them. "Come with me,
children," he whispered. "I've got
something to show you."

Carrying a torch to light the way, Grandpa led the children deeper into the cave.

"Look up there!" Grandpa said, pointing to the cave walls all around them.

"Oh!" gasped the children.
"How wonderful!"

On every side, great painted animals
ran across the walls, with men following
armed with spears and arrows.

"The animals look as if they're alive!"
exclaimed Luli.

"Yes!" gasped Erg. "How did you make
the drawings, Grandpa?"

"Can you keep a secret?" Grandpa asked. Erg and Luli nodded.

Grandpa showed the children his bundles of berries, mud, leaves and wood ash. He showed them how he mixed the ingredients together to make the paint.

"Can we paint, too?" Luli
asked him, boldly.

"Only," said Grandpa, "if you can
think of something important enough
to paint."

The children thought for a moment.

"I'll paint us pretending to be wild animals in the forest," declared Erg.

"And I'll draw the sun shining brightly," decided Luli.

Grandpa chose a place on the rock for them. "This will be a good place for your drawing," he said.

So, Erg and Luli painted tall trees and the shining sun. They painted themselves as wild animals.

The next day, Grandpa brought Ma and Pa to admire the children's work.

"I like those two stripy wild animals," said Pa, laughing. "They remind me of some children I know!"

"The round yellow sun is my favourite," said Ma. "It reminds me that spring will come again. We won't be in the winter cave forever."

"And that," said Grandpa, smiling, "is a very important thing to remember!"

START READING is a series of highly enjoyable books for beginner readers. **The books have been carefully graded to match the Book Bands widely used in schools.** This enables readers to be sure they choose books that match their own reading ability.

Look out for the Band colour on the book in our Start Reading logo.

The Bands are:

Pink Band 1A & 1B

Red Band 2

Yellow Band 3

Blue Band 4

Green Band 5

Orange Band 6

Turquoise Band 7

Purple Band 8

Gold Band 9

START READING books can be read independently or shared with an adult. They promote the enjoyment of reading through satisfying stories supported by fun illustrations.

Penny Dolan enjoys writing stories on her computer at home, and sharing stories with children in schools and libraries. Penny also likes reading, painting and playing djembe drums. She has two grown-up children and one bad cat.

Kirsten Richards lives in a small house near Oxford with her two cats, three plants and more spiders than she'd like to contemplate. When freed from her duties of cat food opener and chin scratcher, she draws and paints to her heart's content.